If a Dolphin Were a Fish

By Loran Wlodarski
Illustrated by Laurie Allen Klein

To the three women who shaped my life – my Mother, Johnnie Ann;
my Grandmother, Helen; and my wonderful wife, Martina – LW
To Bob & Jesse – LAK

ISBN: 978-0-976882329 (hardcover)
ISBN: 978-1-607188612 (paperback)
ISBN: 978-1-607180067 (English eBook)
ISBN: 978-1-934359419 (Spanish eBook)
ISBN: 978-1-60718-252-8 Interactive, read-aloud eBook featuring selectable
English and Spanish text and audio (web and iPad/tablet based)
Library of Congress Control Number: 2005931001

Manufactured in China, May 2016
This product conforms to CPSIA 2008

Arbordale Publishing
formerly Sylvan Dell Publishing
Mt. Pleasant, SC 29464
www.ArbordalePublishing.com

Delfina is a bottlenose dolphin. She lives in the ocean with many of her friends. Delfina often wonders what it would be like to be other animals.

If a dolphin were a fish, Delfina could spend all of her time underwater.

But a dolphin is not a fish. A fish uses gills to breathe underwater. Delfina comes to the water's surface to breathe air through a blowhole on top of her head. Instead of gills, a dolphin breathes air with a pair of lungs.

If a dolphin were a sea turtle, Delfina would lay eggs on the beach.

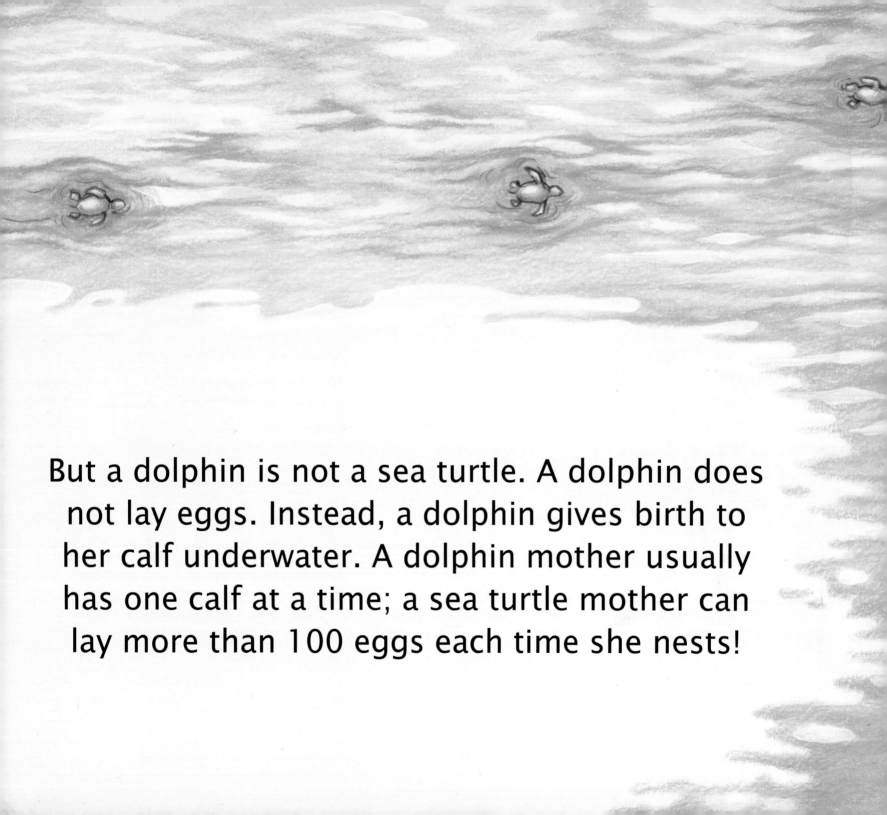

But a dolphin is not a sea turtle. A dolphin does not lay eggs. Instead, a dolphin gives birth to her calf underwater. A dolphin mother usually has one calf at a time; a sea turtle mother can lay more than 100 eggs each time she nests!

If a dolphin were a shark, Delfina could smell her food from far away.

But a dolphin is not a shark. In fact, Delfina cannot smell a thing. Instead, she finds her food with her excellent eyesight and a special kind of hearing called echolocation.

If a dolphin were a manatee, Delfina would only eat plants.

But a dolphin is not a manatee. A manatee eats plants. A dolphin eats other animals, like fish and squid.

If a dolphin were a bird, Delfina would have feathers on her body to keep her warm.

But a dolphin is not a bird. Delfina has a thick layer of fat, called blubber, under her skin to keep her warm in cold water.

If a dolphin were an octopus, Delfina would not have any bones in her body.

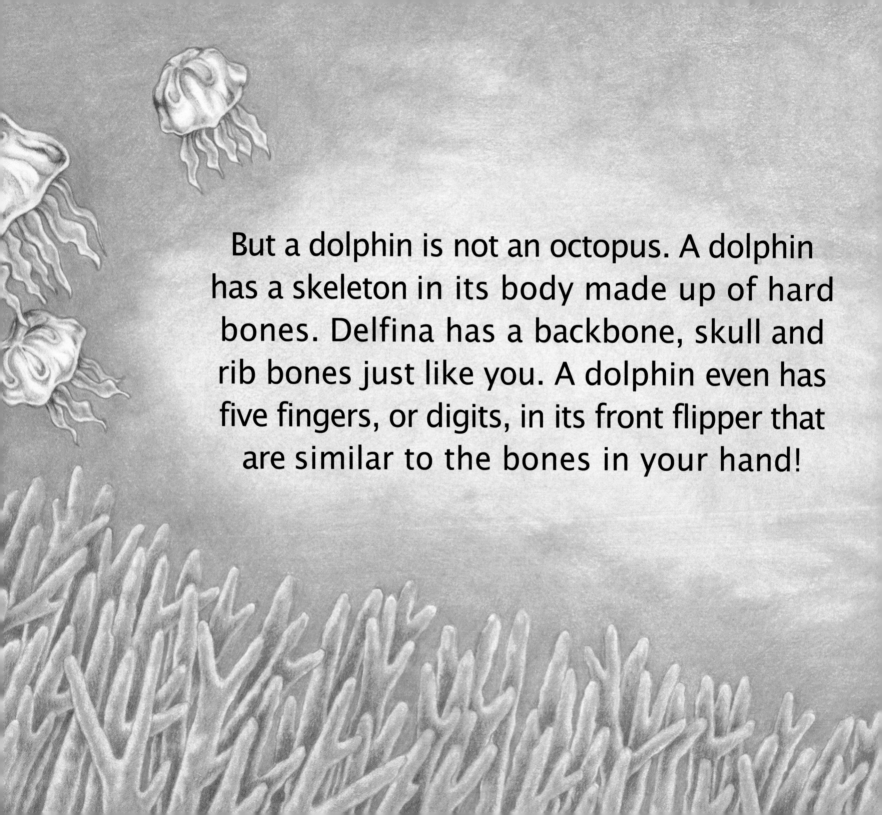

But a dolphin is not an octopus. A dolphin has a skeleton in its body made up of hard bones. Delfina has a backbone, skull and rib bones just like you. A dolphin even has five fingers, or digits, in its front flipper that are similar to the bones in your hand!

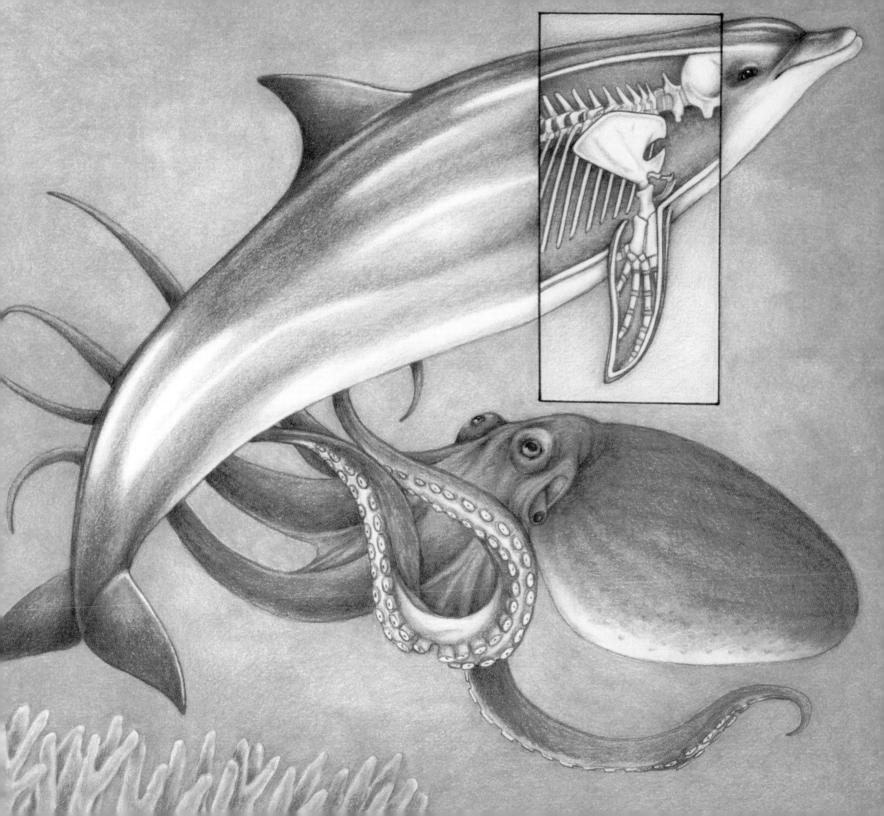

No, Delfina is not a fish, sea turtle, shark, manatee, bird, or octopus. She is a bottlenose dolphin, and we love her just the way she is.

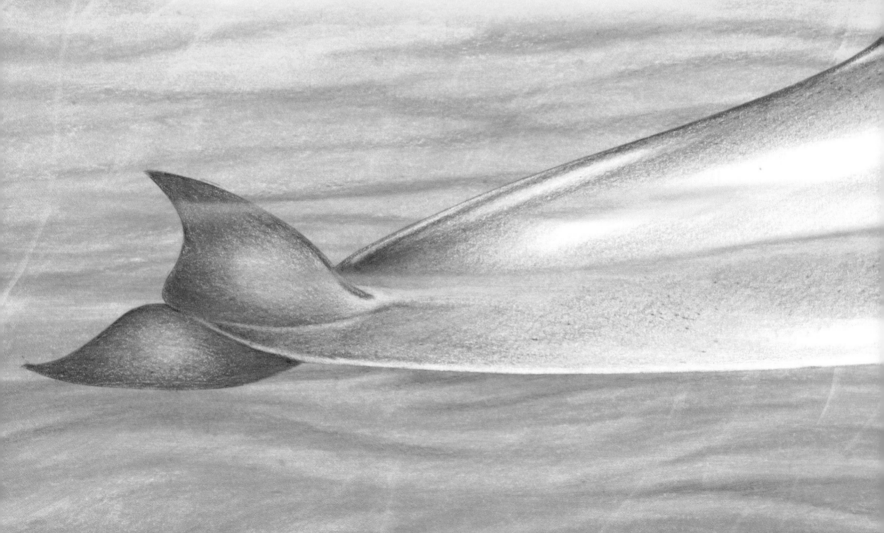

For Creative Minds

The Dolphin Family – Who is Who?

The world is a big place, filled with many types of animals. But, which ones are related to bottlenose dolphins? The closest relatives to dolphins are whales and porpoises. In fact, all dolphins, porpoises, and whales are grouped together in the order **Cetacea**. Cetacea is just a word that means "whale," so dolphins and porpoises are really just small types of whales.

The biggest relative of a bottlenose dolphin happens to be one of the largest animals that has ever lived on our planet — the blue whale. Blue whales can measure up to 110 feet long. Only a few dinosaurs were believed to be bigger. Even baby blue whales, which are about 23 feet at birth, can be larger than a school bus!

How tall are you now?   *How many inches long were you at birth?*

Sometimes people call dolphins **porpoises**, but that is not correct. There are about six types of porpoises in the sea. Yet there are more than 30 types of dolphins in the oceans and five types that live in rivers. The easiest way to tell them apart is by looking at their teeth.

Dolphins have pointed teeth that look like ice cream cones.

Porpoises have teeth that are flatter and not as pointed.

There are many more animals related to bottlenose dolphins and they are called **mammals**. All mammals share certain characteristics or traits.

- They have **hair** on their bodies at some point in their lives. But wait, where is the hair on a bottlenose dolphin? Actually, it all falls off right around the time they are born. Bottlenose dolphins are bald! If you have the chance to look around their snouts (the "bottle" shape at the front of their faces), you'll see little black dots. That's where they used to have hair – sort of like a moustache. Being "bald" helps the dolphins swim very fast through the water. Instead of having hair, birds have feathers – in fact birds are the only animals that have feathers!

- Mostly all mammals have **live birth** instead of laying eggs. The duck-billed platypus is one of the few examples of an egg-laying mammal. Birds and many reptiles (like turtles) lay eggs.

- Mammals **drink milk from their mothers** when they are born. Milk helps mammal babies grow up big and fast. Remember the blue whale baby? A blue whale calf drinks about 130 gallons of milk a day. The calf drinks so much milk that it puts on about 200 pounds of weight each day when it is growing – that's about eight pounds an hour! Bottlenose dolphin babies (calves) drink milk from their mothers for about one year, before eating nothing but solid foods such as fish.

How long does it take your family to drink one gallon of milk?
How long do you think it would take your family to drink 130 gallons of milk?

- All mammals have bones or a skeleton. Our skeleton is inside our body where we don't see it. Some animals, like the octopus or worms don't have any skeleton at all.

- Mammals, birds, and reptiles have lungs and breathe air. Fish use gills to breathe underwater. Bottlenose dolphins breathe through a blowhole on the top of their head. They can stay underwater for 8 to 10 minutes.

  How long can you hold your breath while under water?

- Mammals and birds are "warm-blooded" or endothermic which means that they make their own body heat and maintain a constant body temperature. In humans, that constant body temperature is usually 98.6˚F unless the human is sick. Reptiles are "cold-blooded" or ectothermic which means they use outside sources (like sitting in the sun) to warm themselves. Some mammals also use fur or blubber to stay warm; birds use feathers to stay warm.

  What do you use to stay warm in cold weather?

Do you know any other mammals besides bottlenose dolphins? Cats, dogs, bats, elephants, mice, bears, deer, horses, kangaroos, monkeys, manatees, rabbits, seals, walruses, cows, and sheep are all examples of mammals. Do you want to see another mammal? Look in the mirror! You are a mammal too; so you are a relative of bottlenose dolphin too!

Fun Facts

Dolphins **"hear"** by using **echolocation.** They push sounds out through their **melon** (between their eyes and their blowhole). If you are in or around the water when a dolphin does this, you'll hear what sound like clicks. The sound bounces back off or **reflects** off another object and returns to the dolphin's lower jaw. Dolphins can identify fish, boats and other objects using this special "hearing."

In fact, this "hearing" is so good that they can tell different types of fish apart! Our **sonar technology** is based on dolphin echolocation. Bats, the only mammals that fly, also use a form of echolocation to hear.

Animals that eat only meat are called **carnivores;** those that eat only plants are called **herbivores.** Animals that eat both meat and plants are called **omnivores.**

What are you – do you eat only meat, only plants, or both?

Bottlenose dolphins use their tails to jump as high as 15 feet into the air.

Using chalk on your driveway, sidewalk or playground, measure and draw a 15-foot line.
How many times do you have to lie down (head to toe) to measure 15 feet?
Stand at one end of the line and jump forward.
Measure how far you can jump.

Dolphin Adaptation Craft

Copy or download this page from www.ArbordalePublishing.com and color.
Tape or glue the various "adaptations" to the dolphin as desired.

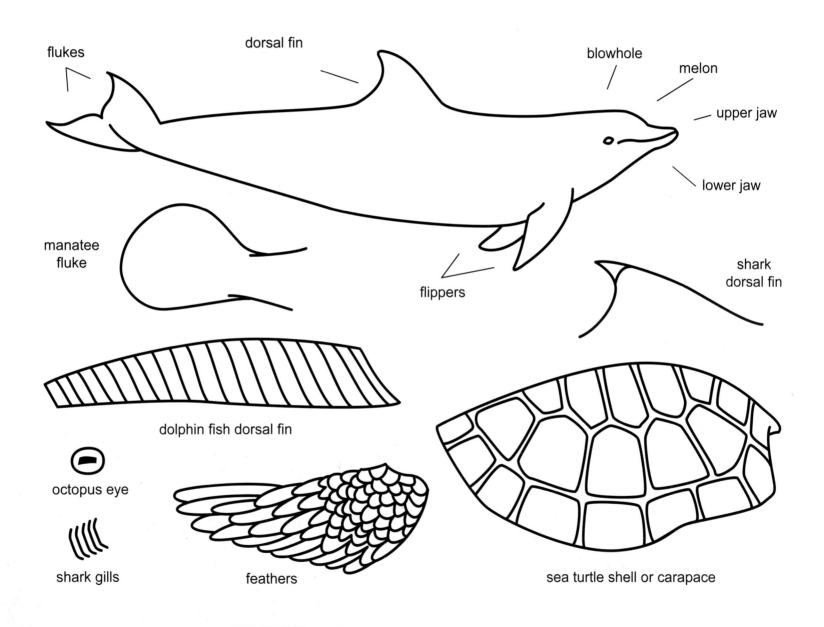

flukes

dorsal fin

blowhole

melon

upper jaw

lower jaw

manatee
fluke

flippers

shark
dorsal fin

dolphin fish dorsal fin

octopus eye

shark gills

feathers

sea turtle shell or carapace